THIS CANDLEWICK BOOK BELONGS TO:

_____

_____

_____

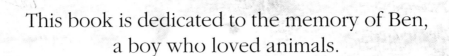

This book is dedicated to the memory of Ben,
a boy who loved animals.

Copyright © 1990 by Sarah Hayes

First U.S. paperback edition in this format 2008

The Library of Congress has catalogued
the first paperback edition as follows:

Hayes, Sarah
Nine ducks nine / Sarah Hayes.—1st U.S. paperback ed.
Summary: As Mr Fox watches and draws closer
to nine ducks, one by one they drop out of sight.
ISBN 978-1-56402-830-3 (first paperback)
[1. Ducks—Fiction. 2. Foxes—Fiction. 3. Counting.] I. Title.
PZ7.H314873Ni   1996
[E]—dc20   95-38453

ISBN 978-0-7636-3816-0 (reformatted paperback)

10 9 8 7 6 5 4 3 2 1

Printed in China

This book was typeset in ITC Garamond.
The illustrations were done in watercolour and ink.

Candlewick Press
2067 Massachusetts Avenue
Cambridge, MA 02140

visit us at www.candlewick.com

Nine Ducks Nine

Sarah Hayes

CANDLEWICK PRESS
CAMBRIDGE, MASSACHUSETTS

Nine ducks nine walked out in line.
Mr. Fox was watching.
One duck ran away, down to the
rickety bridge.

We'll get that fox

Eight ducks eight sat on the gate.
Mr. Fox came through the woods.
One duck ran away, down to the
rickety bridge.

Seven ducks seven took off together.
Mr. Fox came out of the woods.
One duck flew away, down to the
rickety bridge.

Six ducks six did balancing tricks.
Mr. Fox came closer.
One duck ran away, down to the rickety bridge.

Five ducks five began to dive.
Mr. Fox came closer.
One duck swam away, down to the
rickety bridge.

Four ducks four reached the shore.
Mr. Fox came closer and closer.
One duck flew away, down to the
rickety bridge.

Three ducks three flew into a tree.
Mr. Fox came closer and closer.
One duck flew away, down to the
rickety bridge.

Two ducks two had things to do.
Mr. Fox came even closer.
One duck crept away,
to the end of the rickety bridge.

One duck one sat in the sun,
all alone on the rickety bridge.
Mr. Fox came right up close and . . .

Mr. Fox pounced!

The rickety bridge broke and
SPLASH!
Mr. Fox fell into the river.

Nine ducks nine swam back in line.
Mr. Fox went home to his den
and never chased those ducks again.